Fugly Becomes Beauty

A Life Story

Divina Blanco

Ukiyoto Publishing

All global publishing rights are held by

Ukiyoto Publishing

Published in 2022

Content Copyright © Divina Blanco

ISBN 9789360162924

To my father and mother, Celerino and Luz Blanco

Acknowledgement

Many thanks to my husband, Bhanupong; Sister, Celina Blanco-Din; Niece, Pia Katrina Blanco-Mata; Friends: Wadee Deeprawat, Clint Lopez, Pardz Ectin, Lisa Tangsang, Mona Lisa Sangvoranit, Cora Sukhangya, Malou Hoffmann, Susie Paterno Dumont, Tita Evasco Branzuela, Cora Ungab Mesiona, Jocelyn del Rosario Rivera, Carmelita Perales Martinez, and Joey Lim.

Contents

Part 1: Betsy's New World

FuglyBetsy Crawls into a Hostile World

Dawn is breaking in a valley where the silence of the night is broken by a chorus of crowing roosters. Faraway, the thin, pinkish-orange glow of the rising sun is peeking from the surrounding mountains. On the wet grounds, frogs are croaking while crickets are chirping. Somewhere, up on a tree, an early bird is singing loudly, joined by another group sitting on a branch nearby. A couple of owls are flying back wearily to their home to sleep during the day after a night out, looking for prey. In the yard of a house, a dog is barking while chickens in a coop are clacking. In an adjacent meadow, a herd of cows is mooing, waiting for daylight to come.

As the minutes pass, the sun rises slowly over the horizon as its bright yellow rays break the cloak of darkness that enveloped the night before. In a garden, fresh dewdrops stubbornly cling to the leaves and cover the grass. Everywhere, the plants are gradually waking up from their night slumber, anticipating the promise of a new day. In one corner of the garden, nestled on a small branch of a young frangipani, a tiny egg starts to crack.

As the morning sun's rays lengthened, the tiny egg continued to fracture until it had fully opened, spewing a squidgy, moist little green caterpillar.

"Great! I am out of that egg, at last," the little caterpillar said as it tentatively stretched its half-an-inch thin body. "This place does look and feel different," the tiny creature said as its slightly-opened bulging black eyes tried to get accustomed to the brightness of its surroundings while its moist skin started to feel the warmth of the early morning sun and the soft touch of the breeze.

"Welcome to the world, little caterpillar," said Frangipani warmly. "Hello," answered the caterpillar shyly.

Unsure what to do next in unfamiliar new surroundings, the little caterpillar slowly, gingerly shifted her little body; her tiny legs tried to find their footing on the slippery surface of the branch. "One step at a time," the caterpillar began creeping along the length of the branch, looking around, marveling at the sight before her.

"Where am I?" she asked herself loudly. Everything was new to her. Having been inside an egg at the beginning of her life, she feels that the whole place looks immense, frightening, and yet inviting. She had never seen such colors! So many strange things! And she heard sounds new to her ears.

"Well, I'd better find out what is out there," she murmured as she proceeded to amble along the branch. She breathed the air and filled her lungs, hoping her wrinkly skin would become smoother. "It sure is warmer and drier here than inside the egg," the caterpillar said as the sun's rays touched her skin.

"Wow! This place is beautiful!" she observed while continuing to crawl on the branch, her eyes feasting at the sight of green grass, colorful flowers, and the birds, butterflies, and dragonflies that were flying above her. From a short distance, she can hear dogs barking, children laughing, babies crying, and mothers yelling. "My new world!" the caterpillar remarked.

After a while, her stomach started making noises. "I'm hungry," she said. "I wonder what I can eat here, "she said loudly.

"You could start with one of my young leaves," Frangipani answered.

"Really, you are offering me your leaves?" the young caterpillar asked incredulously. "Thank you very much. You are very kind!" she added.

"Oh, don't mention it. You are very small; you won't be able to finish a leaf," Frangipani replied. "Besides, who knows, someday you might be able to help me," she added.

Without any hesitation, the caterpillar bit a tiny piece of the leaf next to her. She chewed very slowly, savoring the new but strange food.

"Super!" the caterpillar exclaimed as it tasted the leaf. "It's delicious! And there is so much food around here!

Hmmn…hmmm, this is good!" the caterpillar said as she continued eating. Still hungry, she consumed some more and more while crawling leisurely along the branch until she reached its end.

"Hey, look out! You're at the end of this branch," Frangipani shouted.

"Oh, no!" cried the caterpillar finding itself unable to go any further. "Where could I go now?" the caterpillar asked itself. Finding herself unable to go any further, the caterpillar looked around her, figuring out where she could go next. "Probably, I can walk back the branch, but I'd like to see what is out there," she told herself. "Perhaps there's another place where there's a lot of food, and there's someone like me." Once more, she looked around her and noticed that there are other plants nearby; some had beautiful flowers. Even close to the ground, there are small plants with flowers. "How I would love to touch those beautiful and colorful things!" the little caterpillar said.

Suddenly, she noticed a pair of menacing eyes staring at her with pure hatred and disgust. Then she heard a shrill, angry voice: "Ugh! Ewww!" screamed the pony-tailed little girl in short pink pants and a white shirt standing nearby.

"Mama! Look! There's an ugly, creepy little worm over here!" The girl yelled, pointing her finger at the helpless caterpillar.

"Creepy! Creepy! Go away! You don't belong here, you ugly thing! Go away, or I'll beat you up!" shrieked the little girl. Quickly, she picked up a long thin branch that had fallen to the ground as she threatened to strike the cowering caterpillar.

"Here I am, you ugly thing!" the girl approached the little caterpillar, now totally afraid, unable to understand what was happening, but it felt the anger and threat toward her.

"Oh, no!" She's going to kill me!" the caterpillar said, shaking in fear. Faced with imminent danger right then and there, the caterpillar pivoted away swiftly, lost her balance, and fell to the branch of a pink Rose.

"Oh, no! You can't stay on my branch!" screamed the Rose with disgust. "Go away, you ugly, revolting, creepy worm! Go away, or else my thorns will rip your stomach!" she shrieked, then started swaying vigorously to get rid of the caterpillar. "I don't want you anywhere near me! You'll just ruin my beauty! I just have this new beautiful bloom, and now you are going to destroy it! It would help if you didn't spoil it with your awful presence on my stem. You'll just drive away those people who like to look at and admire my beauty!" Rose continued angrily.

"Sorry, but I have nowhere to go! Please, let me stay!" the caterpillar begged while curling her tiny body, wishing she would become invisible.

"No! No! You can't stay on my stem! You look terrible! Get lost!" Rose hollered, furiously shaking its body vigorously.

The caterpillar was now terrified and desperate, not knowing where to go or what to do next. It could hardly move, not with all the thorns around.

"Oh! Boy! One mistake and these thorns will surely rip my body open," the caterpillar murmured, quivering in fear.

Just as the Rose began to shake free of the caterpillar, huge, dark clouds moved suddenly across the sky, blocking the sun. At the same time, a gale-force wind blew, causing the little caterpillar to lose its balance falling from Rose's branch.

"Oh! Help!" the caterpillar cried as she fell….

Fortunately, she landed on the back of an old leaf that just happened to be floating by, carried by the strong wind.

"Catch you!" said Old Leaf gladly.

"Thank you, sir leaf," the caterpillar said while catching its breath.

"Markus, I'm Markus," Old Leaf answered as it continued floating above the garden. "And you are?" he asked.

"I am, I am…" the caterpillar answered haltingly. "I don't really have a name yet," it admitted, embarrassed.

"I'll call you Betsy, then," Markus said. "It sounds nice, friendly, sort of breezy," he added.

"Betsy! I like it! From now on, I'm Betsy!" the young caterpillar said happily. "Glad to meet you, Markus! Thank you for rescuing me."

"Don't mention it. I was just passing bypassing by when I saw you helplessly looking for a safe place," Markus replied. "Anyway, hang tight! The wind is getting stronger!" he said.

W-o-s-h-h-h! the wind has become stronger now, forcing Betsy to cling tighter and press herself closer to Markus. She noticed the tiny holes dotting all over Markus's back and the dark spots eating its edges. As the wind continued to blow much more forcefully, taking Markus higher and higher up in the air, above the trees, almost reaching the clouds, Betsy was filled with excitement and fear.

"Oh! Oh! Oh!" Betsy howled in fright. "Hang in there, little Betsy!" Markus shouted back amidst the roaring wind.

From above, Betsy, for the first time, saw many other creatures. There are hens with their chicks, dogs, cats, ducks, geese, and people running for shelter. She also saw many things being blown away, small trees and plants uprooted.

Just as it suddenly came, the wind abruptly died down, dropping Markus on top of a large Mango tree with thick, green leaves, its big branches welcoming them with a massive embrace. Fortunately, the Mango tree is in a stable location, surrounded by many other trees, closer to the mountains, where the air is fresh and cool.

From where they are, Betsy and Markus can see the valley where they just came from.

"Whew! That's a great relief to end up here!" Markus blurted out as he gently unloaded Betsy. "It's very unusual to have that kind of whirlwind during this time of the year when the wind is usually gentle," Markus continued blabbering, still shaken. " The wind was very forceful. I thought I'd fall from your back," Betsy replied with an unsteady voice.

"Well, we are safe now," Markus reassured Betsy. "Let's hope for a calmer time ahead. Great, we are on one of the highest branches of this tree; no human can touch you here," Markus said. "It's a good thing it has no fruits yet to attract anyone. Besides, it has plenty of leaves for you to eat. Hopefully, you will meet someone of your kind to keep you company."

As soon as both of them had relaxed, Betsy asked Markus almost tearfully, "Why do you think the rose and the little girl hated me so much, Marcus? I haven't done anything to hurt them!

"I don't know, little one," Markus answered sympathetically. "Perhaps they don't like anything that is new and looks different from them."

"Am I really ugly and disgusting?" wailed Betsy.

Markus looked at the tiny caterpillar and said, "No, little one. Each one of us is beautiful in our way."

"Really? But why did the little girl and the rose say that I'm disgusting? Betsy wailed.

"They probably didn't know anyone like you before," Markus said, trying to find the right words.

"I wish I was like the rose. She has beautiful colors, and she smells nice. Why can't I just be like the rose," Betsy sighed.

"Listen, little one. You are not ugly. Also, remember that beauty is not everything. There are more important things in this life," Markus replied.

"Like what?" Betsy asked, still confused.

Markus thought for a moment, then said, "Like friendship, love…."

"I don't know those things," Betsy retorted innocently.

"I wonder if I will change when I'm older. Be better looking or be able to do something everybody likes. What do you think, Markus?"

"Ah, I'm sure you will find out later what you are really meant to be," Markus answered. "For now, don't trouble yourself about being beautiful or being someone else. Just be yourself. Don't be impatient. Take each day at a time. Enjoy your life's journey. Make the best of what you have now. Be happy!"

"Thanks for your advice, Markus. I'll try to do as you said," Betsy replied happily. After a pause, Betsy asked, "What about you, Markus? Have you found what you are meant to be?"

"To rescue threatened little caterpillars," Markus replied jokingly. "Seriously, I provide shelter and food to many little organisms, shade to animals and humans, absorb harmful elements in the atmosphere, and many other things for the good of all," Markus said.

"That's wonderful. You are fantastic, Markus," Betsy remarked. "Have you ever experienced being driven away or threatened because of your appearance?"

Not really, my dear," Markus replied. Fortunately, everybody seemed to like trees. Well, that's what my family and I thought for the longest time until...." Markus stopped, then took a deep breath.

"Until when? What happened? Tell me about yourself, Markus! I'd like to hear your story." Betsy said excitedly.

Markus is silent for a while, his mind racing back to those good old days.

Markus Tells His Story

"Do you see the mountains over there?" he asked while turning his body to the direction of a distant mountain range that surrounded the valley. Betsy lifted her small body to look at the place Markus pointed. "Yes. It looks very far from here," Betsy said. "That's where I came from, at the foot of those mountains, quite a distance from this valley," Markus said.

"So, how come you were passing by that garden where I was earlier?" Betsy asked.

"It's rather a long story," replied Markus.

"Oh, please. I would love to hear it!" Betsy begged.

"Well, a long, long time ago, my tree and its family started life there from seeds dropped by passing birds," Markus began.

"You are that old?" Betsy asked incredulously.

"No, not me. My roots, my body, my trunk, and my branches. Do you know that some trees can live for more than a thousand years? But they constantly shed their leaves over their lifetime. Anyway, let me continue," Markus replied.

"Well, I don't really know what a thousand years mean," Betsy admitted shyly.

"Oh, never mind. It means a very long, long, long time," Markus replied, amused. "Anyway, let me go on."

"OK. And I'll be very, very quiet listening," Betsy said, smiling.

"For years and years, there were thousands and thousands of trees in that area near the place where my roots started. But unlike most trees, my tree's family preferred to be on the ground that is a little bit far from others so they could grow very, very tall. Being tall, they attracted honey bees on their branches, making them their homes. For generations, my tree's family had a happy existence. The neighboring mountains were also covered with trees and lush vegetation. It was also home to a multitude of animals, birds, and insects of different kinds. There was plenty of sunshine. The rain came regularly. Plants, birds, animals, and all life forms breathed fresh air. They lived their life as nature planned. All these provided for a happy life for everyone around.

One day, humans came and settled in the valley, not far from my tree's family. They started cutting down the trees in the forest so they could cultivate their own kind of food crops, build their homes, and use wood for fuel to cook, among many other uses. In addition, humans also raised animals like cows for milk and meat. These animals needed a large area for pasture. As the human population grew, more trees were cut down, including those near the valley, for more farmland, for houses, and for many other things humans needed to live. Humans also began to hunt down animals and birds in the forest, uproot exotic plants, and build roads, changing the whole place in the process.

For a very long time, my family trees were spared by humans because of the bees. Humans like the honey that the bees produce, so for years, nobody bothered my family. But, as other kinds of trees were being cut down at a faster pace, the wood-cutters started cutting some of my family members."

"Oh, no! That's bad!" interjected Betsy.

"Yes, it was bad," Markus nodded sadly. "But worse things would come later."

"As time went on, forest destruction and the disappearance of many animals, birds, and other plants are causing the weather patterns to change. It has become more unpredictable. And these conditions affected the life of the bees and made them look for some other place where they felt safer. Little by little, the bees began to disappear.

By the time I came around, my tree was already struggling, fighting destructive insects that eat new leaves like me. "I'm not really old, you know. I used to be dark green and plump. But it's been very hot during the last few months that there was no water to keep my green color. Then tiny insects attacked me for whatever water I still had in me. Gradually, I turned brown, became thinner, developed spots, and grew old prematurely. I've also become too weak to hold on to the stem. Then one day, the wood-cutters finally came. I could still hear them. Markus said his voice breaking.

"Hey, these trees are very tall and big! They would be excellent timber! Let's chop them off!" said one wood-cutter.

"I'm all for it, Buddy," replied the other.

"Yeah, we all are," joined the others as they prepared their giant saw.

"Later, all we could hear was the loud sound of saws and the falling trees until they reached my tree. But as my branch fell to the ground, a strong wind blew and carried me with it. I have been flying around since. Then this morning, I happened to pass by your garden and saw you."

"I'm sorry to hear about your misfortune, Markus. But I'm very thankful you passed my way!" Betsy replied sympathetically.

"That's my life, little one. We never know what happens next," Markus said, looking into the distance. "I am afraid I won't be staying with you for long. I would like to find out if I could still meet my siblings somewhere. Like me, they were blown away by the wind. I wonder where they are now. That's why I have to go soon. Besides, there are so many places that I'd like to see before I wither and die."

"Oh, please, don't leave me here alone, Markus. I don't know what I'm going to do here all by myself," Betsy tearfully pleaded as Markus prepared to leave.

"You will be alright, little one," Markus said, reassuring Betsy. "Besides, being alone will teach you to rely on yourself. Then, little by little, as you go along, you will learn to be brave and daring. You will discover that there is so much in yourself that you haven't discovered yet.

"Thank you for those kind words, Markus. I do hope I will become what you think I will be. I'll miss you, Markus. It's going to be lonely up here with no one to talk to," Betsy said sadly. "Why can't you just take me with you? We can find your siblings and explore the world together. Please take me with you!" Betsy pleaded.

"I'm sorry, little one. I'll have to make this journey alone. I don't really know where I'm going and what dangers I will face along the way. All I know is that I want to go to as many places as I can, for as long as my time would allow," Markus said gently.

"But I don't want to be alone here. I want to go to many places, too. See what is out there. Don't you think it's better to have someone with you to face the world?" Betsy cried.

Before Markus could answer, a strong wind blew him away from the tree, joining other old leaves floating aimlessly toward the ground while dark clouds gathered in the sky.

"Goodbye, dear friend. Take care, dear Markus! Thank you for everything!" Betsy cried out as she watched her friend get smaller until he was completely out of her sight.

Part 2: Betsy And Geo's Amazing Adventures

Betsy Meets a New Friend

"Alone again," Betsy murmured to herself. Betsy surveyed her surroundings and was delighted with what she saw. The Mango tree has many big branches and long stems filled with green leaves. Betsy is on one of the upper branches with a profusion of leaves hanging from interlacing stems and twigs. Looking around, Betsy noticed a young tamarind tree standing nearby, slightly away from the other group of trees. Its branches are thin with only sparse leaves. She is very glad that Markus dropped her on the Mango tree where leaves are green and abundant.

"Great! I'm sure I won't starve here! And there's enough space for me to go around!" she exclaimed. For some minutes, she roamed around her branch, tasting the plentiful green, young leaves. Betsy was just about to take another bite when she suddenly heard a loud deafening sound. B-A-N-G! "What was that?" Betsy asked, trembling in fear, trying to find where that horrible noise came from.

"Relax! That's only thunder," said a calm voice behind Betsy. She turned around swiftly. To her delight, she saw a big caterpillar with dark green skin and a friendly face.

"Hello!" the other caterpillar smiled and greeted Betsy warmly. "I'm Geo." What's your name?" he asked while crawling slowly towards Betsy.

"Hi, I'm Betsy," she replied shyly as the two caterpillars inched closer to each other.

"Finally, I have got company now. I'm very happy to meet someone like you," Geo beamed. "It's been pretty lonely up here being alone."

"I'm glad to meet you, too, Geo!" Betsy replied happily. "How long have you been up here?" she asked.

"I was born here just a few days ago," Geo answered. "There were four of us at first, but the other three fell to the ground."

"That's too bad!" Betsy commented.

"Yes. I really thought I'd be all by myself for the rest of my life," Geo answered.

"Lucky us! Markus, an old leaf, dropped me here. I was also alone at first, and I didn't have any place to go after a little girl saw me and threatened to beat me up because of my appearance," Betsy explained. "And worse, a pink rose wanted to rip my stomach so I wouldn't stay on her branch. She was pretty disgusted with me."

"That's terrible! I can't imagine anyone disliking you. Actually, you look cute," Geo soothed her.

"Thank you!" Betsy giggled, feeling warm inside. "Come, let's go get something to eat," she said.

"Sure. I'm famished, too," Geo agreed heartily. "This place is abundant with food. Just look at all the leaves here! Plenty!"

"Yes. For sure, we won't go hungry here." Betsy said as she started nibbling one young leaf. "What are you waiting for? Let's eat!

"Oh, I just enjoy watching you. I can see that you've got a very healthy appetite." Geo replied teasingly.

"Shut up and eat!" Betsy pretended to be angry.

"Just wait and see. Here I come!" Geo joined Betsy, eating leaves. The two were feasting on leaves around them, enjoying the abundant food when they were interrupted by a terrifying sound…

"Kwak! Kwaak! Kwaak!" "What's that?" Betsy asked fearfully, looking up, trying to find the source. "It's a big bird looking for something to eat. I think we are in great danger. Let's get out of here before he sees us." Geo said, his voice filled with fright.

"But where can we go?" Betsy asked, her little body shaking.

"Hurry, you two!" Betsy and Geo heard their host, Mango Tree, addressing them. "Hide beneath the clump of thick leaves near you. You will blend easily as the leaves have the same color as your skin. Hopefully, the bird won't see you." Mango Tree continued. Quickly, the two caterpillars crawled underneath the clump of leaves.

"I hope we will be safe here," breathed Betsy. "Let's not make any noise. We should be very still," said Geo as the two hid underneath the leaves.

Meanwhile, the bird circled the tree, searching the branches for prey. Finally, it landed on the branch where the two caterpillars were quietly hiding. Threateningly, it surveyed the thick leaves with razor-sharp eyes.

Tock! Tock! Tock! The bird tapped its feet on the branch. "I'm sure I saw two worms here," said the bird loudly. Then it started pecking at the leaves as it walked nearer and nearer to Geo and Betsy, whose hearts were beating fast.

As the two caterpillars settled quietly in their hiding place, Betsy saw something approaching them-a long, dark brown thing, slowly moving toward them. "Hey, look! What's that?" Betsy whispered? "It seemed very scary."

"It's a snake. I hope it won't hurt us," Geo answered. "Be very still." He advised Betsy. "It's coming nearer us," Betsy said in a trembling whisper.

The snake continued to crawl toward the two caterpillars. It was just about to reach them when it caught the attention of the big bird.

"Yeah! My meal!" said the bird. Swiftly, it caught the helpless little snake and flew away with its victim between its sharp beak.

"Whew! That was a close call!" Geo exclaimed as he and Betsy slid out of their hiding place, breathing much more quickly.

"That was really scary!" cried Betsy. "Thank you, Mango Tree, for helping us hide from the bird. You have been nice to us, although we eat your leaves," Betsy said gratefully.

"You are welcome little caterpillars," Mango Tree answered. "That's what I'm here for, to host and feed creatures like you. "I have never seen that kind of bird before," Mango Tree continued. "It must have flown from a forest far away."

"Why did it come here all the way?" Betsy wondered loudly.

"Probably, they are running out of food in the forest because of the extreme heat lately. I've heard from a passing bird that many trees had been chopped down illegally while others burned down because of forest fires brought by extreme heat." Mango Tree explained. "That is why many strange birds are flying out of their natural homes."

"That's terrible! What about here? Has it been hot, too?" Geo asked Mango Tree.

"Oh, yes. We have been experiencing extreme weather for the last few years. Sometimes it gets very hot and dry. Other times, it rains for days. Then it gets very cold. Sometimes the weather changes very suddenly. One minute it is bright and sunny. The next, it gets cloudy and windy, just like today. And it's affecting my health. You can see some of my branches are very thin, and many leaves are turning brown prematurely," Mango Tree replied at length with deep concern. "There are also fewer birds and insects coming this way," Mango Tree added.

 "I've been around for nearly 50 years, and I've never experienced such extreme weather. And typhoons are becoming more frequent and stronger. Two years ago, there was a very strong typhoon that almost uprooted me. It's a miracle I have survived so far!" Mango Tree continued.

"I hope we won't experience that kind of weather," Geo replied, then called Betsy. "Let's not worry about it for now. We'd better enjoy the rest of the afternoon while we can. Let's continue eating while the sun is up. And before it rains. The sky is getting darker."

"I'm still hungry, too!" Betsy agreed as the two crept around, taking a bite from one leaf to another. "This is really great!" Betsy remarked happily.

As darkness came, the winds started to blow stronger again. Betsy and Geo settled quietly in a tiny branch when lightning cut across the night sky like a giant blade, followed by deafening thunder.

Betsy And Geo Survive a Stormy Night

All at once, big drops of water fell. "RAIN!" cried the two helpless caterpillars trying to find shelter among the dripping leaves. "Where could we hide? All the leaves are dripping wet!" cried Betsy, her tiny body shivering. "Let's go back to that clump of leaves where we hid before," Geo suggested.

"Alright," Betsy replied as both crawled ever slowly, trying to find their way back to a clump of leaves. W-H-O-M-M! W-H-O-M-M! W-HO-M-M! The wind was now howling loudly amidst the rain, becoming stronger and stronger as the tree branches swayed wildly from side to side, up and down. Betsy and Geo were soaking wet, clasping each other, when they heard C-R-A-CK! as their branch broke.

"Oh, no! hold tight, Betsy!" Geo yelled at the top of his voice. But before Geo could finish what he was saying, the branch fell, throwing the two caterpillars off-balance, and separated from each other.

Geo was thrown away. "Betsy! Betsy!" he wailed. His voice was lost in the howling wind as he fell down to the water-filled ground. "Oh, no! Oh, no! I've got to go back to Mango Tree. I can't leave Betsy there all by herself!" Geo thought desperately.

"Geo! Geo!" Betsy shouted tearfully, her voice drowned by the thunder. Desperately, she clung to the branch that now has dropped to a bigger branch near the ground.

"Betsy! Betsy!" he cried out her name over and over, hoping she would hear him. Geo couldn't see anything in the darkness. His eyes were blinded by the falling rain. The rainwater is taking him farther from the tree. "No! No! I can't be separated from Betsy! I have to find her." Geo kept telling himself as he struggled to find a way back. Fortunately, the branch has fallen next to the Mango Tree blocking the flow of water and enabling Geo to climb back slowly.

"Geo! Geo! Where are you?" Betsy bawled loudly but heard nothing except a chorus of "C-R-O-A-K! C-R-O-A-K! from frogs below.

After some time, exhausted and wet, both Geo and Betsy fell asleep amidst the downpour. As dawn came, the rain finally stopped. Unknown to both, they are just a few feet away from each other.

With the sun brightly shining, Geo and Betsy woke and saw the destruction around them. There was debris all around. Branches of trees fell while flowering plants were uprooted. Dark, murky, and dirty water floods the ground below.

"Where could Geo be?" Betsy asked herself while looking down. "There's still rainwater on the ground, so many leaping frogs around, and lots of fallen leaves and branches," Betsy wondered. "What if Geo is on one of those leaves? What if the water takes him farther away, to a river? How can he climb back and find me? I hope frogs don't eat caterpillars." Betsy started to cry, thinking of the worst.

Meanwhile, Geo continued looking for Betsy. His heart beat fast when he saw the branch beside him look very similar to the one where they were before the rain. "That looks like our branch," Geo said to himself, trying to sound hopeful as he moved slowly toward it.

"I hope Betsy is here," Geo said to himself, creeping faster and faster. "Betsy! Betsy! Where are you? Betsy! Betsy!" Geo kept calling.

Betsy is also moving anxiously, not knowing what to do next. "Should I jump down or go up or across to another branch?" she wondered aloud. Then all of a sudden, she heard a familiar voice calling her name. "Betsy! Betsy!"

"Geo, Geo! I'm here!" Betsy answered back at the top of her voice. Relief filled each other's hearts as they rushed to meet each other. After navigating the slippery branches, the two finally met. They hugged each other tightly and joyfully.

"I thought I have lost you," they said simultaneously, then embraced each other again. "What a night it was!" Betsy said. "Yes, we just had a very terrifying time yesterday and night," Geo agreed.

"At least we have learned that there are predators out there. And bad weather happens anytime," Betsy replied.

"And we both survived by being there for each other," Geo commented.

"Let's keep it that way," Betsy replied.

"Good morning, young lovers!" Mango Tree greeted them gladly.

"It's a beautiful day! Although I lost a branch, I am delighted the rain finally came. Look, my leaves are fresh and green! Enjoy them. Have your fill."

"Thanks, Mango Tree!" Geo said. "We are surely starving to death after last night's fright."

"Yes! It's now time for our breakfast. After last night, I can only think of eating," Geo announced.

"Me, too!" Betsy agreed. "I can eat tons of leaves right now."

Without delay, the two started binging on leaves for the rest of the day until they were so full that they could hardly move.

After the storm, pleasant days followed. Days were sunny, and nights were cooled by gentle breezes. The two grew bigger and bigger as their appetite for green leaves seemed to be limitless. As their size expanded, they started shedding their skin to accommodate their expanding bodies.

"Aren't you bored doing what we have been doing for

days now?" Geo asked Betsy one morning while they were nibbling fresh, young leaves. "We've already gotten very fat, and we're shedding our skin all the time."

"Well, I don't know…I feel secure up here. Nobody is bothering us," Betsy answered, having a good time eating leaves.

"But perhaps we can do something else," Geo said. "Like what?" Betsy asked, slightly annoyed.

 Geo thought for some moments but could not think of anything new they could do while they were up on the tree. "Well… I don't know," he finally said.

And so, for the next few days, they keep on consuming leaves, creeping from one branch to the next, looking for younger, softer leaves. At night, they slept below the stars. Sometimes they see a group of fireflies glowing from tree to tree.

"Wouldn't it be fantastic if we could fly…" sighed Betsy wistfully. "But there's nothing else we can do here but eat, eat, eat. And I'm getting very fat!"

"Ha! Ha! Ha! Me, too. We are a couple of fatsos!" Geo laughed.

One morning, Betsy was surprised to see Geo busy doing something. It looked like he was spinning some thread from twigs nearby and then weaving them into a sleeping pad.

"What are you doing, Geo?" Betsy asked. "You do look very busy all of a sudden."

"Oh, it's nothing!" Geo replied coolly. "I'm making a sleeping pad where I can sleep undisturbed."

"Why? Do I disturb you at night? Betsy asked, annoyed. "Should I move to another branch away from you so you will have peace?"

"No! Betsy!" It's nothing like that! You know I love to have you around all the time," Geo said soothingly. "It's just that I want to have a long, undisturbed sleep. I have a feeling that I'll be different when I wake up," he added.

"Well, I might do the same thing later," Betsy said. "But I'd like to continue eating for a while. I'm always hungry."

"Fatso, Betty!" Geo teased as he joined Betsy to eat more leaves.

"Hey, do you think when we wake up and we look different, would we still recognize each other?" Betsy asked, a bit worried.

"Oh, I'm sure we will, Betsy. We will always be together," Geo said, hugging Betsy.

"I do hope so, dear Geo," Betsy replied happily, then continued eating leaves while Geo worked on his pad.

Betsy And Geo Sleep Long

The following day, Geo finished his sleeping pad. "Betsy, I think I'm ready for my great sleep. Please take care of yourself while I'm sleeping. Pretty soon, you'll be sleeping, too," Geo said while hugging Betsy goodbye.

"I'll miss you, Geo. Dream of me," she replied, already feeling sad.

"Sure, I'll see you in my dreams, dear friend. But I have to go now," Geo answered as he attached himself upside-down to his sleeping pad. After a short while, Geo swung and twisted gently to get rid of his old skin. Then, he became quiet, sleeping soundly. Betsy observed him for some moments. "Hmmm, I wonder how he can sleep that way," she thought.

The next day, Betsy went to see Geo hoping that he would be awake and already out of his sleeping pad.

"Hmmm, he is sleeping soundly. I should not disturb him," Betsy said, feeling slightly disappointed. "I wonder if he will be fatter with all that sleep! Well, I better make my sleeping pad right now. I can hardly wait to see what it's like to sleep for days."

Betsy worked on her sleeping pad most of the day while taking some time to do what she and Geo used to do, non-stop eating until they were so full that they could no longer move. "I have to finish my sleeping pad soon, so I can experience what Geo is experiencing right now," Betsy told herself as she continued spinning silk threads to make her pad.

Suddenly, Betsy felt very alone. She missed Geo and wished he was with her right now, enjoying the leaves that she was chewing while making jokes that never failed to crack her up. But now, there's only silence except for the soft whispers of the wind and the occasional tweeting of birds. Longing to be close to Geo, Betsy crept near his sleeping pad again.

"I miss Geo. I'd better go and have a look at him once more before I go to sleep, "she murmured. She stared at the pad, wondering if Geo was dreaming about her. As she kept looking at the pad, Betsy noticed that a green shell appeared underneath Geo's old skin. "Oh, that's pretty strange. I wonder why his pad is changing its color by itself. How would he look when he wakes up and emerges from that shell?" Betsy asked herself. At night, she stopped working, lying alone on the branch, looking at the stars, and wishing Geo was around.

The following day, Betsy saw that the green shell had hardened but remained hanging silently on the branch. "Good! My pad is nearly done! I can hardly wait to see what it's like to sleep for days. Geo seemed to have disappeared completely," Betsy thought sadly.

Betsy continued working on her sleeping pad. "I need more silk thread, she said. I should work harder and faster so I can finish my pad as quickly as I can."

Later that day, Betsy's silk pad was finished. "I'd better hang my pad next to Geo, so we won't miss each other when we wake up," Betsy quipped as she hung her sleeping pad right next to Geo. She was now ready to sleep. Before she got in her pad, Betsy looked around her, taking everything in her memory. She wondered if everything would still be the same when she woke up. She crept up and down the branch and took one last nibble of a few young leaves.

 "I hope to see you again, Mango Tree. You have been very kind to Geo and me," Betsy told their host, Mango tree.

"It's a pleasure having you here. I would be very happy to see you again soon. I am sure you will find wonderful new things when you wake up. As you will see later, life is full of mystery and surprises." Mango Tree replied.

"I do hope so, Mango Tree. I have a feeling it's going to be a whole new life when I wake up," Betsy said. As she prepared to attach herself to her sleeping pad, she was filled with a sense of adventure and, at the same time, some fear of the unknown. Then, she completed the steps that Geo had done just a few days before. Finally, Betsy is inside her sleeping pad next to Geo.

For the next couple of weeks, the two sleeping pads hung quietly on the branch, swaying in the breeze, occasionally twitching slightly. Unknown to the sleeping caterpillars, they underwent a life-changing transformation that only Mother Nature could perform. Inside their sleeping pads, their caterpillar bodies break down into newer parts. Their colors are also taking different hues and unique designs.

Part 3: Betsy and Geo's World of Wonder

Transformed!

One morning, Betsy's sleeping bag finally opened. Feeling squeezed for a long time, she emerged weakly. "Hmm, that was quite a sleep!" she said, stretching her body. "What! what happened to me?" She asked, feeling something very different. "Oh, my, my, goodness! I have a pair of wings!" she cried out in amazement. "I have been transformed into a butterfly!"

"Now, I can fly!" she excitedly spread her bright yellow, black, white, and orange wings. "I wonder how I look," Betsy mused. She tried to flap her wings but could not, for they were still weak and heavy. Disappointed, Betsy waited for some minutes before trying her wings again. She failed once more. After another try, instinct made Betsy draw fluid from her abdomen to fill her wings. After such a difficult act, Betsy needed time to rest and gather her strength. After a few hours, which seemed like an eternity for Betsy, her wings felt stronger. This time her wings worked.

"Super, now I can fly!" she hollered jubilantly.

Betsy was about to fly when she glanced upward, feeling a pair of eyes watching her. "There's someone up there watching me," she murmured. She stared back at the other butterfly, sensing that she knew him.

"Could it be? But that butterfly is blue," she thought excitedly, her heart beating fast. To her great joy, the blue butterfly called her name.

"Betsy, Betsy! It's me, Geo! Didn't I promise you that I would be here waiting for you?" the blue butterfly called Betsy joyously.

"Geo! Geo!" she cried. "It's great to see you!" Thrilled, she spread her wings and flew straight to Geo. "How long have you been waiting here?" she asked emotionally.

"I've been here watching your pad for two days now. I can hardly wait to see the new you. And you turned out to be so beautiful, Betsy!" Geo said and kissed her sweetly.

"And you are good-looking yourself! Isn't it great we can fly now?" Betsy exclaimed with pure delight.

"Absolutely! It's a new life! A new adventure for us!" Geo agreed.

"This is fantastic! We can fly, see everything and smell all the flowers in the garden!" they shouted. And the two continued their flight, sometimes at a very high altitude, then flying close to the ground, fascinated with everything they saw, touched, and felt. Giddy with joy, Betsy and Geo prepared to fly away from Mango Tree when it started swaying its branches while calling them, "Hey, you two! Don't forget to help me bear fruit! It's been so long since butterflies flew up here," Mango Tree added.

Embarrassedly, the two butterflies stopped and shyly assured the host tree, "Of course, we will! Thank you very much for your hospitality, Mango Tree! Helping you bear fruits is the least we can do to pay you back!" Betsy and Geo responded simultaneously.

"See you later, Mango Tree! We'll be back soon!" the two new butterflies cried out as they flew away.

Ecstatic to begin their new life and the seemingly endless adventures waiting for them, the two butterflies flew away. At first, they circled the ground below, looking at the garden, wondering where to start.

"Yeah! Isn't this great! We can fly and smell all the flowers in the garden!" they shouted.

"Before we go to the garden, let's explore other places first. We might discover many new things along the way." Geo suggested.

"Alright! I would like to see the whole wide world!" Betsy agreed gleefully! Without wasting time, the two soared up the sky, then dropped to the ground like a pair of kamikazes.

"Hey! Why don't we fly to that mountain over there?" Geo shouted.

"Sure, I was just about to say that," Betsy shouted back. "I would like to see where my friend, Markus, the old leaf, came from. I hope it is not too far for us to fly."

"Let's see how far we can go and how high we can fly. After all, we wouldn't know if we didn't try," Geo answered.

"OK! OK! No lectures, for now, Sir!" Betsy replied jokingly.

As they climbed up the sky, they saw plants and animals that they had not seen before. From their vantage, they saw humans doing their everyday work. Farmers in their farms heard of cows eating grass in the meadow. They noticed small children playing on the ground and many other sights fresh to their eyes. They also heard sounds that they had never heard in their previous life.

As they passed the valley, Betsy saw very tall trees. "Come, let's take a look if some of those trees are Markus' relatives," she said.

"How would we recognize them," Geo asked. "I guess if honey bee hives are hanging from their branches, that would be them," Betsy answered unsurely.

For some minutes, the two butterflies flew near tall trees until they spotted one with bee hives. "Come, let's check out that tree with bee hives over there!" Betsy pointed excitedly. When they reached the tree, they rested on one of the branches.

"I'm sure this tree is Markus' relative. The shape of its leaves is almost the same as Markus's. I'm thrilled to be able to see where Markus came from. Betsy said amid the buzzing of thousands of honey bees flying around."

"Good! I'm glad to see this place, too." Geo replied. "Shall we continue our journey now?"

"But of course!" replied Betsy happily.

As they approached the mountains, they saw smoke from a far distance and bright sparks coming from its direction. Farther away, they can see orange-yellow flames devouring trees and everything else along their path. The flames seem to be moving down the mountains to another remote valley.

"Oh, no! That's forest fire!" exclaimed Geo. "Let's not go there! It's too dangerous!" Right then, they saw birds flying away from the burning mountain. Down below, they can see herds of animals running wildly in search of a safer place.

"That must be what Mango Tree told us. No wonder that strange bird had to escape and find a new home," Betsy said. "Let's go somewhere else, then."

The Amazing Rainforest

As the two changed course, they observed that a massive part of the mountains was still covered with tall, big trees with long branches and a canopy of dark, massive, green leaves. Geo and Betsy can see many birds flying on top of the trees, having the time of their lives. As they neared the mountains, a fantastic sight greeted them.

"Look! It's massive water falling from the mountain! How wonderful it looks! Betsy shouted. That place is gorgeous! Come, let's go near the waterfall."

From afar, the waterfall looks like a three-step staircase carved on a mountain draped by a curtain of cascading white water. It is so vast that it seems to cover half of the mountain and so high that it touches the sky. The first tier drops into a large pool of blue water that looks like an overflowing basin dotted with islets and huge rocks. From this giant pool, the water falls into smaller pools, separated by huge rocks hanging on the edge of the gigantic basin. These smaller falls course down the mountain into a number of rivers that flow in many different directions.

The sides of the waterfalls are covered with lush vegetation, including an assortment of beautiful wildflowers of different colors. There's a multitude of birds and perhaps thousands of butterflies flying over and around the falls.

"Come, let's go over the waterfalls!" Betsy was giddy with delight. "I'm with you!" Geo shouted back.

The two flew across one of the rivers and rested on one of the protruding rocks. Looking at the river bed with huge white stones at the bottom, its crystal-clear water reflecting the clear blue sky, the white cirrus clouds, and the reflection of giant trees around, Betsy and Geo saw their images for the first time.

"That must be us!" exclaimed Betsy. "Yes, that's us," Geo confirmed.

"I must say we are beautiful!" Betsy said proudly. "Yes, we look like the perfect picture with the blue sky, the bright sun, and everything around us!" Geo agreed heartily.

Savoring the beauty around them, they turn their attention elsewhere. They wanted to see more of their world when they visited, above to their left, high up on the trees, a large multitude of brightly colored butterflies flying around.

"Look! Our relatives over there! cried, Betsy. Excitedly Come, let's say hello to them!"

Swiftly, the two flew and mingled with thousands of butterflies of different shapes and colors. "Hey! We haven't seen you two before! Said a dark blue butterfly addressing Betsy and Geo. Its wings look similar to Geo's, only bigger and darker.

"We are new here; we came from the valley, " Geo replied. "Have you been here all your life?" he asked the white butterfly.

"I've been here for the last couple of days," the blue butterfly replied. "I actually came from the far side of this mountain range. The one that is now burning. Perhaps you noticed the smoke and the sparks."

"Yes, we did. At first, we wanted to go that way, to explore as far away as possible from where we came from. To see what is really out there in this world," explained Betsy.

"Do you know how the fire started?" Geo asked the white butterfly, who by now is joined by others.

"Well, I am not really sure. But my friends here and I saw humans the other day. They have been cutting many trees in the last few years, leaving the ground exposed to the hot sun. The ground there has become very dry, and the grass and shrubs have been dying because there's no more canopy to shade them from the hot sun. Probably, that's how the fire started. It's a good thing we could escape just when the fire started," the blue butterfly continued.

"Lucky us. We were able to get away," a yellow butterfly chimed in. "I saw many birds burned in the fire. They must have been sleeping when it happened."

"Not only birds. I saw many animals on the ground, unable to escape," said a bright yellow-green butterfly, her wings shining in the sunshine.

"Good thing we found this place. It's simply beautiful!" said a red and white butterfly.

"Yes, it is," Geo and Betsy agreed. "We'll fly around here and explore the place."

"We'll do the same," chorused the others.

So, Betsy and Geo flew around, savoring the sound of the water plunging down the pool below and the sweet melody of birds singing many tunes. Then to their delight, a rainbow appeared, reflected across the waterfall.

"What a perfect sight!" the two butterflies shouted their pure admiration.

"Why don't we go down that gigantic pool to see what's in it?" Geo asked.

"Let's go!" Betsy agreed.

They saw huge rocks rising from the pool's bed as they flew down. "Let's rest on one of those rocks," Geo suggested. "Good idea! I'm a bit tired, too," Betsy concurred.

As the two were resting on one of the huge rocks, they noticed the water's clarity. They could see a different kind of fish swimming contentedly. On one of the rocks, they saw a huge tortoise sleeping contentedly while its partner was swimming leisurely nearby.

For some moments, the two silently took in the sights and sounds around them, the loud drop of the water to the dark blue pool and the soft, soothing warbling of the river flow. Hundreds of monkeys are jumping up on the trees from one branch to another, making funny sounds. At the same time, birds of wide varieties sing or call their mates. Down below, deer and wild boars are playing on the forest floor below.

"Can't we stay here forever? This must be what a paradise is like," Betsy blurted.

"Yes, we could, but don't forget we promised Mango Tree that we'd help her bear fruits. We must go back," Geo told Betsy.

"I know. We have to keep our promise. But can we at least spend the night here and perhaps another day before we go back to Mango Tree," Betsy agreed. "Of course we can, my dear," Geo replied gladly. "But right now, I'm starving. Let's go to the jungle to find something to eat." "OK! I'm starving, too. After that long flight, I can definitely eat a ton," Betsy agreed.

"Let's find an ant's nest or a ripe fruit somewhere among those trees. "This place is very huge. We don't know where to start," Geo observed.

"Well, if we are looking for ants' nests and eggs, we can start on the ground. I hope we can find red ants," Betsy said.

"Good idea!" Geo replied. Then the two flew away from the waterfall pool nearer the ground, covered with undergrowth of giant ferns, forest floor shrubs, and other flora, many with flowers.

"Hey! We can get some pollen from those flowers," cried Betsy. "Yes, of course!" agreed Geo. And in no time, the two dropped into a couple of forest flowers, tasting their nectars.

"Good! Good," both said simultaneously. "But I'm still hungry!" said Betsy. "I know. You have a huge appetite," teased Geo as they flitted from one flower to the next. "Just be careful we don't get near flowers that trap insects."

From time to time, the two saw snakes slithering on the ground and others climbing on trees. "This place is pretty exciting. "Geo noted. "It's a good thing we now have wings. We can fly away any time if we want. "Nature's gift to us," smiled Betsy.

After flying around for a while, the two spotted a fruit that had fallen on the ground and was attacked by thousands of red ants.

"Look! I just saw what we are looking for," Geo exclaimed. "Oh, no! I'm not eating rotten fruit or red ants!" Betsy retorted.

"No, we are not eating either. We'll observe and follow the red ants to their home so we can find their nest," Geo clarified.

"Excellent idea!" complimented Betsy as both flew, following the ants closely until they reached their home, where they settled close to their nest, now filled with eggs.

With one quick swoop, Geo and Betsy swallowed many ants' eggs filling their hungry stomach, then hastily flew away.

"That was fun!" Betsy said, laughing. "Our first meal as butterflies!"

"Yeah! It's great!" Next meal, let's try fruit," Geo suggested.

By then, the sun is already setting. Darkness is slowly creeping across the horizon. Birds and animals in the forest are rushing to find their way home to rest for the night.

"Let's have another meal before it finally dark," Betsy recommended. "I agree," Geo replied as the two flew around the nearby trees, searching for some fruit.

"Hey! Look at that monkey! He is eating something!" pointed Betsy after flying around.

"Yeah! There's plenty of ripe fruits hanging on a tree over there!" happily said.

Immediately, the two flew straight to the ripe fruits and had their fill. "Gosh, I'm sure I'll have a good night's sleep with my full stomach," Betsy remarked satisfactorily. "Let's go back to the waterfall. I want to experience a night with the waterfall serenading me to sleep."

"We have a fantastic first day, don't you think?" Geo said as the two settled on the top of one of the big rocks protruding on the waterfall pool as they listened to the rhythm of the falling water hitting the bottom of the fall below. "I couldn't agree more," Betsy replied.

The night was pitch dark and starless, but the trees were alight against the backdrop of total darkness, with millions of fireflies hovering on their branches.

"Look! Isn't that fantastic! All those tiny twinkling lights up on the trees!" Betsy called out in pure delight. "Truly, mesmerizing," concurred Geo." Now let's go to sleep.

The morning had just broken when the forest was filled with a cacophony of sounds, waking up Betsy and Geo.

"Kwaak! Kwaak! Kwaak!" shouted the birds while flying up in the air. "Kwik! Quick! Hip!" hollered the monkeys as they swung from one tree branch to another. "Hoo! Hoo! Hoo" cried some animal below. "Tweet! Tweet! Tweet" birds chirped in various melodies.

"Good morning! The forest noise woke me up!" Betsy exclaimed. "Sure, it's different here," Geo laughed.

"OK, now, "Let's take things easy on our way back and enjoy our journey," Geo said.

"I was just about to say that," Betsy uttered as the two flew again to the tree with ripe fruits for breakfast. "There's nothing better than a good, sweet fruit for breakfast," Geo said. "Yes, now I'm ready for our trek back to the valley," Betsy replied.

"Let's follow one of the rivers that flow near the valley. We haven't seen that place yet. Who knows what we'll see along the way," Geo proposed. "Gladly," replied Betsy.

Following the river from up the second-tier pool, Betsy and Geo again saw the majestic drop of the water with the bright morning sun shining. They met several butterflies again on their way to their destination in other directions. Different kinds of birds are flying up across the sky.

"Hey guys, called one of the butterflies. Where are you going?"

Betsy And Geo Do Their Work

"We're going back to the valley," Betsy and Geo replied in unison.

"Why? The forest is much better for us. No humans, yet. We can live as we please. I've heard the valley is full of humans; many are not friendly to us."

"Well, we made a promise to our host tree, so we are going back," Geo explained.

"Good luck then. We are flying to the back of this mountain. We heard it's more beautiful there and more abundant food." The blue butterfly said.

"Good luck!" cried Betsy and Geo as they continued to fly down along the river path. From time to time, they flew up and down the length of the falling water down the pool, then back up to the sky before flying closer to the river, where they found a multitude of wildflowers growing near the bank.

"Oh, boy! Aren't these flowers gorgeous!" cried Betsy as she flitted from one flower to another, drinking their nectar and collecting their pollens. "Indeed, they are," Geo nodded in agreement as he drank nectar.

"Hey! I see beautiful flowers up on those trees, too! Let's go have a look."

Clinging on the branches and trunks of the trees is a profusion of orchids. "Wow! Look at these flowers," exclaimed Betsy. "They resemble us, don't you think?" Their petals are shaped like our wings."

"Yes! And their colors are magnificent, pink, white, blue, yellow, and violet." Geo observed.

"It's so beautiful up here. I keep repeating myself," Betsy said. "But duty calls."

"You are right. Let's get going, or else Mango Tree might think we have forgotten about her." Geo said. "Alright, alright!" Betsy replied a bit grudgingly as they continued their journey along the steep course of the river down the mountain. Their senses are filled with the sights and sounds of the forest and the soft gurgling of the river as the water hits stones and rocks along the way. Occasionally, they saw fish jumping out of the water, perhaps to catch a mosquito or a fly to eat.

"Look! That fish can fly!" observed Betsy. "Unbelievable."

"Strange and fantastic!" Geo agreed. "The forest is really amazing. I wonder what else we would see along the way."

After some time, the river winds down along the plain.

"This place is different now. I don't see flowers or tall trees with flying monkeys anymore. Not even birds and our fellow butterflies. The plants are all the same, planted in neat rows," Geo said as they flew over hectares and hectares of maize.

"Yes, it sure is different," Betsy replied, looking at a scarecrow in the middle of the fields. "Do you see that place over there?" she asked, pointing to another place, a long distance from the river toward the direction of the forest fire they had seen a day before.

"Yes, I see it. It looks totally devastated," Geo replied. "Come, let's have a look."

As they flew, they noticed that the air had become hotter and heavier, and the land below was almost barren with sandy soil. Only a few straggly trees dotted the area where the grass was thin and short. "This place looks desolate," observed Geo. "Yes. It looks like there are no animals, birds, or butterflies here," Betsy agreed. She saw a small white butterfly flying toward the mountain as she spoke.

"Why are you here?" asked the white butterfly. "This place is almost abandoned. Nothing here for you! I'm going up the mountains where life is better and where my family went ahead of me. My family has been here for a long time, but things have changed a lot in the last few years. At first, I wanted to stay, hoping things will change for the better, but they only got worse."

"What happened here?" Geo asked.

"According to my parents and their parents before them, this place was part of the forest, filled with trees and animals. Then humans came and started clearing the land, cutting trees, and driving away all the animals.

The land was converted into farms. At first, the farms thrived. But in recent years, forest fires are often due to extreme heat. The fires extended down to this area, burning almost everything in sight. I was in another area, quite far from here, but things there are turning into something like this place. Just yesterday, the fires came, almost burning everything. Luckily, I escaped just in time."

"Thank you for telling us. We are not going to stay here for long. We are just passing by on our way back to the middle of this valley. By the way, the mountains are truly great. You will like it there." Geo replied as they proceeded to the valley.

As they continued their journey, Betsy and Geo passed by a pond not far from the valley. "Come, let's rest near the pond, drink some water and find something to eat," Betsy offered. "Hungry again!" Geo joked. "Sure, I can use a bit of rest, and the pond looks inviting."

"Yeah, we can sit on that big stone at the pond's edge," Betsy replied.

While resting on the stone, a toad jumped near them. He looked alarmed and fearful. "Don't drink this water!" he warned them. "Somebody nearby has just sprayed some herbicides. It's poisonous, you know. I'm going up to the river."

"Thank you, toad, for warning us!" Geo and Betsy said together as they watched the toad hop away.

Garden Flowers in Despair

Meanwhile, in nearby flower gardens, the plants are getting restless. The weather has been erratic, as it has been for the last few years. Worse, in one garden, the owner has been spraying the fruit trees with chemicals to keep insects from eating their young fruits. In another park near a busy road, exhaust and gasoline particles pollute the air. At the same time, another garden is kept meticulously clean with almost daily mowing. Thus, butterflies, bees, and birds are rarely around this year. It is the beginning of spring when flowers are supposed to bloom, but most plants haven't been pollinated yet. There was an air of gloom and worry everywhere.

White Gardenia is panicking. "I'm getting old. Still, I'm unable to bear flowers," she complained to Marigold, her neighbor who is also filled with dread at the thought of not blooming this year. "I would love to bloom again, one last time, before I'm finally too old to have flowers," lamented Gardenia.

"Don't be silly, Gardenia. Your kind has a very long life. It seems to me that you can live forever." Said Marigold. She, too, is getting on years. She worries that the garden owner might uproot her and replace her with a younger one. Unlike Gardenia, Marigold has a more delicate body that needs to consume water regularly to survive.

"You will be alright, Marigold," Gardenia said encouragingly. "We only need a bee or a butterfly to pollinate us."

"Yes, it's early spring now. We need to be fertilized before summer, or else we'll miss the chance to bear flowers this year," Marigold replied.

"We also need rain before it gets too hot," said Dahlia.

"Yes, but not a storm we had a couple of weeks ago. I thought I would die that night," replied Bougainvillea. "All I want now is to bloom while there's plenty of sunshine."

"I do wish my garden owner would stop spraying that awful chemical for once. It's driving away our butterfly and bee friends," complained Gardenia.

"I wish these vehicles running around us would stop polluting the air. I could hardly breathe, so do the bees and butterflies," said Passionflower, straddling the fence of one garden and another.

"I agree," said Hibiscus. "I've been waiting for some bee or butterfly to come around for days. I used to bloom the whole year round, but now, I'd be lucky if I bloom even once."

"I feel the same way as you do, Hibiscus. I haven't bloomed for months now. I wonder if I still have my scent," white Jasmine joined in.

"I'm afraid it's getting too hot for me to survive," complained Calla Lilly. "The other day, my owner almost forgot to water me. I thought I'd die of thirst. Like you all, I'm desperate to have flowers soon."

"We have two problems now, the heat and the absence of pollinators," Angel's Trumpet chimed in from the neighboring garden. "Over here, my gardener is always mowing the lawn. There's nothing left for tiny insects to hide. No food for bees, butterflies, and birds. "

"What should we do then? I'm pretty desperate now," African violet cried.

"Me, too," said tiny Begonia.

"We all are," chorused all the flowers.

Just then, Geo and Betsy flew over the garden.

"Hey, look! Our wish has just been answered. I see two butterflies above!" Dahlia exclaimed. "Fantastic!" the flowers cheered in unison. "Let's invite them here!" they shouted as they started to sway, trying to attract the attention of the two butterflies.

Nearby, a Tamarind tree heard them and waved her leaves forcefully, trying to attract the two butterflies. At the same time, Bird of Paradise flapped her massive leaves.

"Please come here and help us!" howled the flowering plants.

"Hopefully, I will have flowers and later bear fruits with the help of these butterflies," Tamarind said optimistically.

Not far from them stood Frangipani, also wishing to have flowers soon. She, too, started waving her branches to catch the butterflies attention.

"Hey, butterflies! Over here!" the plants called Betsy and Geo, who noticed the frantic waving and shaking of the plants in the garden. "Hey, Betsy! Look at the plants in the garden. They seem to be calling us," Geo observed. "Yes," Betsy agreed. "It looks like the garden where I came from, but I don't see any flowers this time. Let's see if Pink Rose is still there," she added. "OK! Let's go check them out," Geo replied.

"Oh, well. It's getting dark. Let's come back tomorrow instead," Betsy said before they reached the flowers. "I agree. Let's find something to eat, then we go back to Mango Tree to spend the night there," Geo replied.

"Good idea. I can use some food myself. I'm tired and hungry already," Betsy remarked as they flew away from the garden.

"Oh, no! The butterflies are flying away from us!" cried Marigold. "Probably they didn't see us because we don't have blooms," Gardenia lamented.

"Probably they smelled the chemicals my garden owner just sprayed," complained Hibiscus.

"Listen, everyone! Let's wait for tomorrow. Who knows, they might be back," Bird of Paradise sounded hopeful.

"I agree with you, Bird of Paradise. Let's hope for another day. Right now, I'm just going to sleep and dream," Jasmine said.

Away from the flowers, Geo spotted something on the ground. "Hey Betsy, I think I saw a fruit over there. Let's go check it out."

Quickly, the two flew down and found ripe papaya. "This is fantastic!" exclaimed Betsy in delight as they sucked the sweet sugar from the fruit.

"Now we can go back to Mango Tree," Geo said, satisfied his stomach was already full.

As twilight unfolded, the two finally reached Mango Tree. "Hello, Mango. We came back as promised," Betsy greeted their host tree.

"Welcome back, my friends," Mango Tree replied. "It's so good to see you, not to mention that I felt some pollens that you carry dropped on me."

"Promise kept," Geo remarked happily. "Now, we'll go to sleep. It has been a long day."

 "It will be another exciting day tomorrow. We'll go back to the garden to visit those flowerless plants," Betsy said. "But before we see them, let's go back near the river bank where we saw wildflowers. We need more pollens to spread over those plants in the gardens."

"You are absolutely right, Betsy," Geo agreed.

As soon as dawn came, Betsy and Geo woke up to start a new day. "It's great to wake up to see the sunrise, don't you think?" Geo asked Betsy as they flew over the fields and farms where animals were waking up.

"Oh, yes! And I can't wait to be back on the river bank with all those marvelous flowers. We can even find an ant nest for breakfast," Betsy replied happily.

As the early morning light brightened the horizon, Geo and Betsy reached the river bank and dove straight to the bed of wildflowers filling their tiny feet and abdomen with pollens while sucking nectar as much as they could.

"I'm so full!" cried Betsy. "We can go back to the garden now."

"Let's go then before it gets very hot," Geo nodded.

It was almost midday when Geo and Betsy reached the garden. The plants looked sad and weary.

"It's almost the middle of the day, and yet there's no trace of those two butterflies we saw yesterday," a disappointed Calla Lilly observed.

"Things are looking worse," tiny Begonia agreed.

"Hey! Look! I see something up there!" Angel's Trumpet joyfully announced. "The two butterflies are back!"

"Oh, yes! Super!" the plants chorused. "Let's call them!"

From above, Geo and Betsy could see the plants swaying vigorously, their leaves and stems flapping gently in the breeze. Immediately, the two butterflies flew down. "I will go down this garden," said Geo. "And I will go to that garden where I came from," Betsy answered as the two flew separately. Geo and Betsy stopped by each plant and dropped some pollens.

"Hello, you!" They greeted each plant.

"Thank you very much for coming to our garden," Gardenia welcomed Geo. "My pleasure." He answered. All the plants greeted Geo and Betsy in a similar way. All were grateful for their presence.

In the other garden, pink Rose is standing alone quietly. Like the other plants, she is also desperate. But she is just too proud to join in the conversations. She saw Betsy flying above, but she did not want to do anything to catch her attention.

"I'm a rose. Everybody wants to please me," pink Rose said to herself. "I'll wait here until that butterfly sees me. I'm sure she will come."

Betsy first went to see Frangipani, her former host. "Hello, Frangipani! It's me, that little caterpillar who crawled on your branch a few weeks ago," she greeted Frangipani.

"My little friend! You have become such a beautiful butterfly!" exclaimed Frangipani.

"Thank you for your kindness, Frangipani. Now it's my turn to pay you back," Rose said as she dropped pollens all over Frangipani.

"Thank you very much, my little friend. Come back anytime you like," Frangipani replied happily.

"I'll see you around, Frangipani. I'll have to visit other plants," Betsy answered as she flew away in pink Rose's direction. She is about to land on pink Rose when she realizes she has already used up all her pollens. "Well, I'll just come back tomorrow," Betsy told herself.

"Oh, no! she is not going to come to me," pink Rose quietly cried as she saw Betsy flying away. "I'll have to do something to catch her attention," she said as she began to sway frantically. But Betsy was too far by now to notice her.

The next day and the next, Betsy and Geo followed the same routine of getting up at dawn to collect pollen from the wildflowers near the river bank, then back to the gardens. For three days, Betsy and Geo flitted endlessly among the plants in the garden.

"Super! I'm drunk with nectar every day! I can live forever like this!" Geo happily remarked one early evening as he and Betsy rested on one of the branches of a Mango Tree.

"I'm happy Mango Tree also received some pollens from us," Betsy answered.

"Yes, I have," Mango Tree replied, overhearing Betsy. "I'll have flowers soon, and if nature is kind, I'll have fruits by summer." Mango Tree added happily. "I can't wait to see your flowers and fruits, Mango Tree, "Betsy said.

The following day, Betsy and Geo once again flew around the garden when to her surprise, Betty heard haughty pink Rose say, "What a pair of beautiful butterflies!"

"Hello, Rose!" Betty said as she stopped by pink Rose and dropped some pollens. "I bet you don't recognize me, "she continued.

"I'm sorry. Have we met before?" Rose asked, confused.

"We've met before, a few weeks back. I was a little, ugly caterpillar that landed on your branch. You threatened to rip my stomach open if I stayed." Betsy answered.

"I'm sorry for being so mean," pink Rose replied. "Please forgive me." She added.

"I forgive you. Now I must go. There are many other plants waiting for me and my partner, Geo," Betsy said, then flew away.

On the ground, Betsy saw a group of young children playing. She flew near them and saw the pony-tailed little girl who hated her so much. She nearly killed her. The little girl looked up and saw Betsy and Geo flying and flitting among the flower plants.

"Hey, look," the little girl called her friends. "Do you see those two beautiful butterflies near the flowers?" she asked them. "Common, let's catch them!" she yelled. She and her friends immediately ran toward the two butterflies, intent on catching them. Before the children got near Betsy and Geo, the two butterflies flew away quickly.

"Too bad they are gone!" the pony-tailed girl wailed. "I wanted to catch them for my collection. I think they are perfect!" she said sullenly.

"Why don't we try to catch them tomorrow?" said one of the little boys in her group. "We can put a ripe fruit in the garden to attract them. So, while they are eating, we can catch them with our net," the little boy continued.

"Good idea! Until tomorrow then," the pony-tailed girl replied gladly. Before she could finish talking, drops of rain started falling. "Rain! Let's go home," the children shouted as they ran to their homes.

It rained heavily the rest of the afternoon and well into the evening, providing much-needed relief to the parched garden and drenching plants to their delight.

The Flowers Bloom

Days later, the garden started to be filled with colors. Gardenia is radiant with her white, sweet-scented flowers just beginning to appear. "Look, I'm blooming!" she exclaimed happily.

"I'm just thrilled. I'm flowering at last," Marigold beamed as her tiny, bright yellow-orange petals began to show themselves.

In another part of the garden, Dahlia's purple, pink and light-yellow blossoms also attract onlookers for their majestic look. "Goodness, everybody is looking at me," Dahlia quipped proudly.

"Me, too," admitted pink Rose as she displayed several pink buds." Many thanks to those two butterflies who came over here."

On the ground, Daisy's flowers are all over. They come in red, yellow, orange, and white colors. "Aren't my flowers simply gorgeous?" she beamed.

Over on the fence, Passionflower is beginning to bloom. Soon she will show her white petals with a blue ring in the middle surrounded by purple filaments. "Good! Now I can spread my sweet scent for everyone to smell. Then by mid-summer, I'll bear fruits for everybody to enjoy," she said proudly.

"Oh, I know. Very soon, everyone will admire my orange blossoms that look like trumpets from heaven," Angel's Trumpet declared proudly.

"Passionflower, you are not the only one who could fill the air with scent," commented an annoyed Jasmine. "Me, too! Humans can make garlands with my blossoms that they can take everywhere."

"But I can make this neighborhood so beautiful more than anyone else!" boasted Bougainvillea. "I have very dark red, white, orange, pink, yellow, and white blooms!"

"Not so fast, Bougainvillea! You are not the only one with many colors! I, too, have orange, yellow, and red flowers," objected Hibiscus.

"Common, guys! Everybody will see me first because I'm the tallest, with the largest leaves," a gleeful Bird of Paradise boasted, her bright orange and red blossoms starting to show.

"But everybody loves me because I'm cute and delicate," little Begonia smiled with her pink blossoms.

"Just like me," joined African Violet, her purple blooms spreading on the ground.

"Enough of this boasting," an exasperated Calla Lilly shouted, her dark orange and red flowers turning brighter. "Let's all be happy we are all blooming now."

"Amen to that," everybody said in happy agreement.

Nearby, Tamarind tree burst happily, "I'm very heavy with flowers now. I'm carpeting the ground with my white petals. I'll surely have tons of fruits in summer."

"So am I," a satisfied Frangipani joined the overjoyed group of flowers in the garden. "My pink flowers are coming out!" she said aloud.

Everywhere in the garden, the flowers and trees are dancing in the wind, filled with happiness as their wish to bloom comes true. The flourishing gardens attracted bees, birds, and other butterflies as they enjoyed frolicking and flying there. In the process, helping more plants to glow with life.

Part 4: Betsy And Geo's Story Goes On

Betsy Finds Her Purpose

Exhausted but satisfied, Geo and Betsy flew back to Mango Tree to rest and reflect on their accomplishment. "Well, I think we have done what we are supposed to," Geo said.

"So, this is what our life is all about. This is what Markus told me to find my purpose in life- to help make our world beautiful and to help others live," Betsy replied happily.

"Not too fast. There's one more thing we must do," Geo said, looking at Betsy's eyes intensely. "And what is that?" Betsy asked with a shy smile on her face.

"To have our own little ones, of course. So, they can carry on our work," Geo said, embracing Betsy. Sweet and tender moments followed, sealing the love of the two caterpillars for the rest of their time together.

Days later, Betsy started to feel strange again. Her stomach was becoming heavy, and she couldn't stop eating just about anything she could find. At times, she feels like throwing up every time she eats. Worse, she gets thirsty very often as dew drops evaporate quickly these last days of spring. As summer days are fast approaching, days are becoming warmer with the sun's rays getting stronger. Nighttime is not much help when it becomes very humid. Each day is scorching, hotter than the day before. All creatures are becoming thirsty while plants in the garden are parched. Their leaves are turning dry and almost brown. They are all hoping for rain.

"It's hard to find succulent leaves around here," Geo observed one morning. "Yes, and I need to eat more good leaves these days," Betsy agreed.

"The leaves in the lower branches are farther from the sun's heat. They are still green and succulent, attracting tiny insects that we can eat. Let's go down a couple of branches," Geo suggested. "OK, let's go," Betsy replied.

With her growing stomach, Betsy flew down very slowly to a lower branch. "Oh, I'm so tired, and it's hot. Can I rest for a minute" Betsy said, catching her breath.

"Take your time, sweetheart. Don't exert too much effort these days. You need to conserve your energy." Geo comforted Betsy. "Anyway, we're almost there. Once we find a good place to settle, you can rest and eat."

Resting for a few minutes, they continued their slow flight down to a lower branch. After what seemed an eternity for Betsy, they found a spot in a lower branch with a canopy of thick green leaves providing them a shield from the hot sun and plenty of food.

"I think this place is perfect for us. It's cool, and I see crawling tiny insects everywhere," Geo said. "I agree,"

Betsy replied, feeling exhausted. "Now I can rest comfortably."

"Gosh, I can hardly move," Betsy said while chewing the food Geo fed her. The next couple of days, Betsy rested and ate most of the time as she grew bigger.

"Geo, Geo, come over here, next to me," Betsy called out loudly one morning. There was a slight panic in her voice. "Betsy, what's wrong?" Geo flew quickly to her side. "I think I'm going to release my eggs now," Betsy replied, her voice quivering.

"What should I do?" Geo asked nervously, hovering around Betsy. "Just stay close to me, Geo," she said as she calmly waited for the right time to release her eggs. She felt cramps in her stomach, contracting every now and then.

Later, Betsy inhaled and repeatedly exhaled until two tiny eggs came out of her body first. One egg is light blue. The other is light green. "Look, Geo, our eggs!" she gasped, relieved and happy. "Betsy! You are great!" Geo shouted joyfully, fluttering all over Betsy. He looked at the two eggs proudly and flew around them proudly.

"Oh! Wait! I think more eggs are coming out!" howled Betsy in excitement. Again, she inhaled and exhaled repeatedly. Soon, she released another egg. This time, it is light pink. Then another, a white one. Two more followed, a yellow one and an orange one.

"We have six eggs in total!" exclaimed Geo happily. "Isn't that fantastic! You are the greatest, Betsy! I love you!" Geo was overwhelmed with joy as he kissed Betsy and the newly-released eggs. Just then, he noticed how quiet Betsy was. Greatly alarmed, he saw Betsy had turned very pale, drained of color. Her wings lay flat.

"Betsy!" he screamed in panic. "Are you alright?"

"Geo, I'm exhausted, and the heat is killing me," Betsy whispered to Geo, catching her breath. "Releasing six eggs drained my strength." She said haltingly. "I'm very, very tired. I want to rest." By now, Betsy can hardly open her mouth. "Please take care of our little eggs. Put them in a safe place." She gasped, feeling her life slipping away.

"Betsy! Betsy! Be strong! Stay with me!" Geo cried out while holding the dying Betsy. "Please, please..." he pleaded.

Betsy is now struggling to keep her eyes open as she tries to say something, "Goodbye, Geo, my love. It has been a wonderful journey with you. Please look after yourself, too," she whispered weakly. She tried to raise her wings to embrace Geo for the last time, but she could not. After a few more labored breaths, Betsy closed her eyes, never to open them again.

"Oh, no, no! Betsy," Geo wept, shaking her gently to keep her awake. "You can't leave me here all by myself! "How can I take care of these eggs you left behind?" he cried tearfully. After a long time, Betsy became rigid, and her body started to turn cold.

"Geo, I'm sorry about Betsy," Geo heard Mango Tree's comforting voice. "But remember, everything in this world has a beginning and an end. At the same time, be grateful for your time with Betsy. Her memory will sustain you the rest of your life," Mango Tree continued. "I will help you protect the eggs until they hatch. Keep them where they are now."

Grief-stricken, Geo covered Betsy lovingly with his wings. "I'll join you soon, my love," Geo addressed Betsy.

Tenderly, he moved Betsy's lifeless body to a safe corner of the branch with abundant leaves. Later, he moved the six eggs next to Betsy, three on each side like little honor guards. For hours, Geo sat next to Betsy, watching her and remembering the first time they met, how they enjoyed eating all those leaves around. He smiled sadly at the thought of Betsy's joy when he reassured her that she looked cute. His mind recaptured all those precious moments they shared together: those moments when they hid among the leaves, holding their breath, very frightened that the big, black bird would find and devour them. Then, later that night, a storm came. His heart could still feel his anguish and terror at the thought that he had lost Betsy when they got separated. He recalled those days when they didn't do anything but binge on food. Then that glorious moment when they turned into butterflies after what seemed to be forever inside their cocoons.

"Betsy, Betsy, why did you have to go so soon," Geo said softly, heartbroken. "It wasn't so long ago when we were so happy at our transformation. You were very beautiful, and you enjoyed flying, fluttering, and flitting among the plants. And you have a big appetite." In tears, Geo smiled, remembering how Betsy loved to eat.

Evening came. Geo still hasn't moved away from Betsy's body. He remained there all through the night, keeping vigil with the lonely moon as his distant company. Geo must have slept when he was awakened by a rooster crowing far below. A sad new dawn is unfolding. When the sun came up, Geo stretched his wings and prepared to fly away. Before he left, he kissed Betsy goodbye.

With a heavy heart, Geo at first decided to fly far away from the garden where he and Betsy spent so many days together. The thought of seeing those familiar plants was just too much for him. They reminded him so much of Betsy. Yet, he thought that by seeing those flowers in bloom, he would see Betsy in them. With his broken heart, he flew down the gardens.

In the bright sunshine, he saw how beautiful the flowers had become. He imagined Betsy flying all over them, greeting each one with her warm smile, fluttering her wings on the petals. He wished with all his heart that Betsy was with him, enjoying the splendor they helped create. He noticed that Tamarind had dropped almost all its flowers to the ground, creating a white carpet around its trunk. "Tamarind is bearing fruits already," Geo observed as he noticed small fruits emerging all over Tamarind's branches and stems. "How I wish Betsy could see those tiny fruits."

Geo circled around the gardens for a long while, observing how the plants were flourishing despite the heat. Then he decided to say hello to Frangipani, remembering that Betsy had started her life on its branch.

"Hello, Frangipani," he said. "I can see you have so many beautiful pink flowers.

"Oh, yes! Thank you!" Frangipani replied, smiling, as her flowers gently swayed in the gentle breeze.

"I'll visit pink Rose before I go. It's a good thing she drove Betsy away. If she didn't, we probably would not have met," Geo said to himself, flying straight to pink Rose. For a brief moment, Geo landed on one of pink Rose's flowers. Its petals are soft, a lovely shade of pink, and smell so sweet. "I wish Betsy could smell this scent. She would have loved it." Geo's heart is now heavy with grief. "I've got to get away from this place, now," he said, then flew swiftly away. "I have to go somewhere where there's nothing to remind me of Betsy.

For hours, Geo aimlessly flew until he saw a meadow. It looks so calm and serene, a comfort to his pain. He could hardly see any flowers or trees, just a sea of tall green grass dancing gracefully in the wind. He decided to rest for a while among the grass, watching dragonflies hovering above a buffalo grazing alone. He listened to the birds singing and crickets chirping.

"It is so peaceful here," Geo said to himself. Briefly, his grief somewhat eased that he fell asleep.

"Take care, Geo," he heard Betsy and felt her kiss. "Betsy! You are here!" he cried, opening his eyes, hoping to see Betsy, but she was not there. "It was only a dream. I wish I didn't have to wake up," Geo murmured, broken-hearted. His sorrow heightened when he looked around and saw at a distance a pair of butterflies flying up in the air, having the time of their life. He felt acutely what he had lost. A gust of cold wind blew, reminding Geo how alone he was that he decided to fly back to Mango Tree. With darkness creeping, Geo flew fast until he reached Mango Tree, utterly exhausted. His energy was totally spent.

"Try to sleep, Geo. Think of the eggs. They will open any day now. Don't you want to see your offspring?" Mango Tree tried to console Geo.

"I don't know, Mango Tree. I don't know any more what I want in this life," Geo said, still inconsolable.

A New Life Cycle Begins

That night, the heavens opened, and rain came. It kept pouring for days on end. All this time, Geo stopped eating, remaining motionless beside Betsy. One morning, Geo noticed that Betsy's body was gone. There was only a trace of her yellow wings imprinted on the branch. Devastated, Geo lay down on the place where her body once was. He tenderly moved the six eggs into a neat row. Finally, in the midst of a heavy downpour, overcome by grief, Geo breathed his last.

A few days passed as the rain continued pouring. Then one morning, the rain stopped, and the sun finally came out. One by one, the eggs rolled slowly to the middle of the branch, then stopped. A little while later, the eggs simultaneously cracked. One by one, a tiny, squidgy caterpillar emerged. Squinting, they looked around first, then at each other. "Strange new world," they said to each other simultaneously. All six of them observe one another. Three have dark green skin with black lines circling their bodies and yellow dots next to the dark lines. The other three have light yellow-green skin with black and white lines circling their body.

"Hello," they said to one another. "Who are you?" they asked each other at the same time.

"Where are we? Asked one caterpillar. "What is this place?" asked another one.

Before any could answer, they felt the rustling of the leaves around them and heard a comforting voice, "Welcome to the world, little ones," it was Mango Tree who had been watching over them since they were eggs. "I am Mango Tree, your host. "You can stay here for as long as you want, just like your parents did. You are free to eat my leaves and crawl wherever you like." Mango Tree continued, "You are brothers and sisters. You do look exactly like your parents," Mango sighed. "Before everything, I should give you names. First, you should all move to form a row. from left to right. The farthest left I will call Clint, the second, Suzy; the third, Leni; the fourth, Sam, the fifth, Joey; and the farthest to the right is Jenny. Step forward when I call your name, OK?"

"Clint!" called Mango Tree loudly. Little Clint crawled forward, his dark green body still moist. Then Mango Tree continued calling the names of the caterpillars.

"Suzy!" little Suzy has light-green skin. She crawled slightly faster than Clint.

"Leni!" she is tinier than Suzy, but like her, she has light-green skin.

"Sam!" he has dark green skin like Clint's, but he has white and lines circling his body instead of just black.

"Joey!" he looks almost identical to Clint; except he is shorter and fatter.

"Jenny!" She is the smallest among the six. Like Suzy, her skin is light-green.

"Excellent! Now we have names!" exclaimed the little caterpillars gleefully as they merrily crawled around one another.

"Now run along. I have other things to do. But always be careful. There might be birds or large insects that like to eat worms and caterpillars like you," Mango Tree said, sounding like a doting grandmother. "I'm also starting to bear fruits, so there might be more tiny insects for you to eat."

Left to themselves, the siblings looked at each other and smiled, wondering what to do next.

"Good morning, sisters and brothers," they chorused. "Let's play," Clint announced, acting like their big brother.

"Let's go, everybody. Let's explore this branch," answered Suzy, the second in command.

"But before we play, I hear my stomach grumbling. I think I'm hungry. Could we get something to eat first?" Leni asked.

"Me, too," squeaked tiny Jenny.

"I am hungry, too," Sam declared.

"We are all hungry," Joey said.

"Of course, my dear siblings. I was just about to say the same thing. Let's get something to eat." Clint answered.

And in the bright sunshine, under a blue, cloudless sky, side by side, the tiny caterpillars crept slowly and tentatively on the branch, instinctively nibbling the nearby leaves. Their life adventure has just begun the same way as it has for their parents, as it has always been since the beginning of time.

About the Author

Divina Blanco

Divina is an ex-banker and a climate finance specialist. She likes to write stories in her spare time. This is her first published story.